BIG and Noisy Simon

Joseph Wallace

Illustrated by
Kevin O'Malley

HYPERION BOOKS FOR CHILDREN · NEW YORK

Printed in Singapore
FIRST EDITION
1 3 5 7 9 10 8 6 4 2
This book is set in 16-pt. BlueJack.

LIBRARY OF CONGRESS CATALOGING-IN-PUBLICATION DATA
Wallace, Joseph E.
Big and noisy simon / Joseph Wallace; illustrated by Kevin O'Malley.—1st ed.
p.   cm.
Summary: Simon cannot help being big and noisy, until he goes
to Africa with his parents and watches a herd of elephants being
big and noisy sometimes and silent when they need to be.
ISBN 0-7868-0515-3 (trade)—ISBN 0-7868-2450-6 (library)
[1. Self-control—Fiction. 2. Elephants—Fiction.] I. O'Malley, Kevin, 1961– ill. II. Title.
PZ7.W15675Bi 2001
[E]—dc21   00-35022

Visit www.hyperionchildrensbooks.com

For Shana and Jacob, of course.

–JW

Everybody liked Simon.

It was just that he was so big. Bigger than anyone else in his class, even the girls.

Simon was also noisy. He was as noisy as he was big, and that made him very noisy.

Sometimes when he was big and noisy, nobody noticed.

But mostly when he was big and noisy, people complained. "Simon, please try not to yell," said Simon's parents; his little sister, Annie; his teacher; and even his friends. Or they would say, "Oh, Simon, look where you're going," or "Watch out for that glass!" Simon wished that he weren't always so big and noisy. Everyone told him just to be patient. "You'll grow into your body," they said. "You'll learn to speak more quietly."

"When?" Simon asked. "This summer?"

"We hope so," everyone said.

Simon's mom and dad were photographers. They took pictures of birds and animals for magazines. To get close to the birds and animals, they had to be very quiet and careful.

Simon didn't usually get to go along.

But this summer was different. This summer, the whole family was traveling to Africa, where Simon's mom and dad were going to photograph lions, giraffes, monkeys, and other animals.

First they had to take a long plane ride. Simon decided that during the plane ride, he would try not to be so big and noisy.

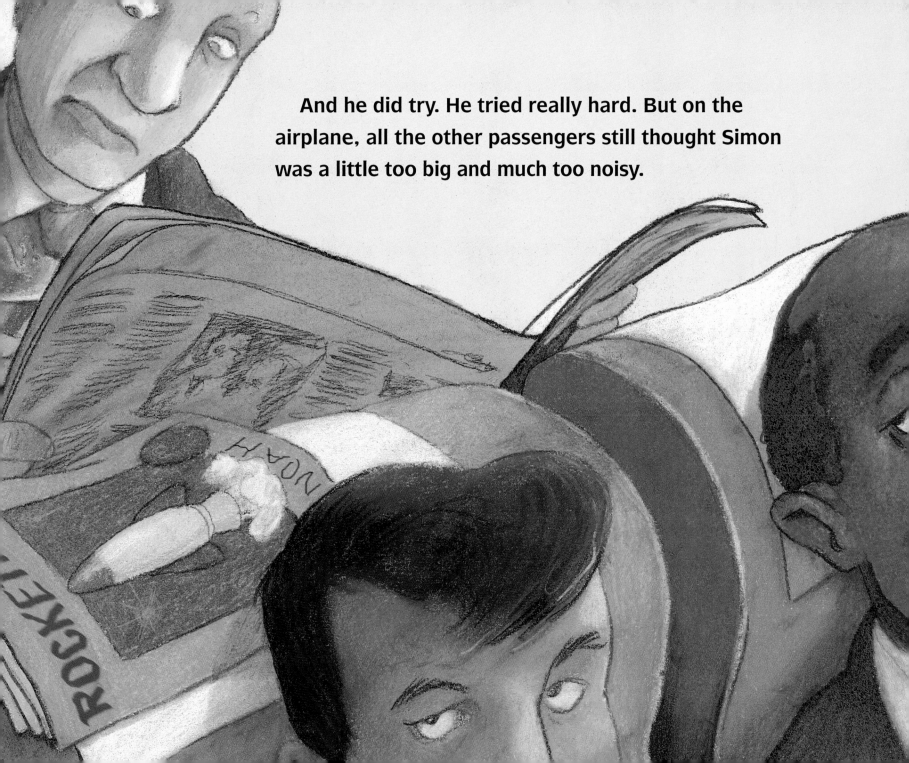

And he did try. He tried really hard. But on the airplane, all the other passengers still thought Simon was a little too big and much too noisy.

In Africa, Simon and his family stayed in a house surrounded by grass that seemed to go on forever. Everywhere Simon looked there were animals. Even before he unpacked, Simon saw zebras, giraffes, wildebeests, and warthogs.

The next morning, Simon's mom and dad asked if Simon wanted to come when they went out to take pictures. "These birds and animals don't see very many people," they said. "So we all have to be quiet when we watch them."

"I'll try," Simon said.

And he did try. He tried really hard.

Ahhhhh . . .

But he was noisy when they saw antelopes and gazelles.

He was big when they went to a lake and found some crocodiles.

And he was especially big and noisy when they visited a whole family of lions.

He was bigger than the noisy vervet monkeys. He was noisier than the tall, quiet giraffes. Warthogs, ostriches, impalas, buffalo, waterbuck, hyenas—Simon was bigger than all the noisy ones, and noisier than all the big ones.

The next time his parents went out, Simon didn't get to go along. Now he knew that he wasn't just bigger and noisier than anyone else in his class, but in all of Africa, too.

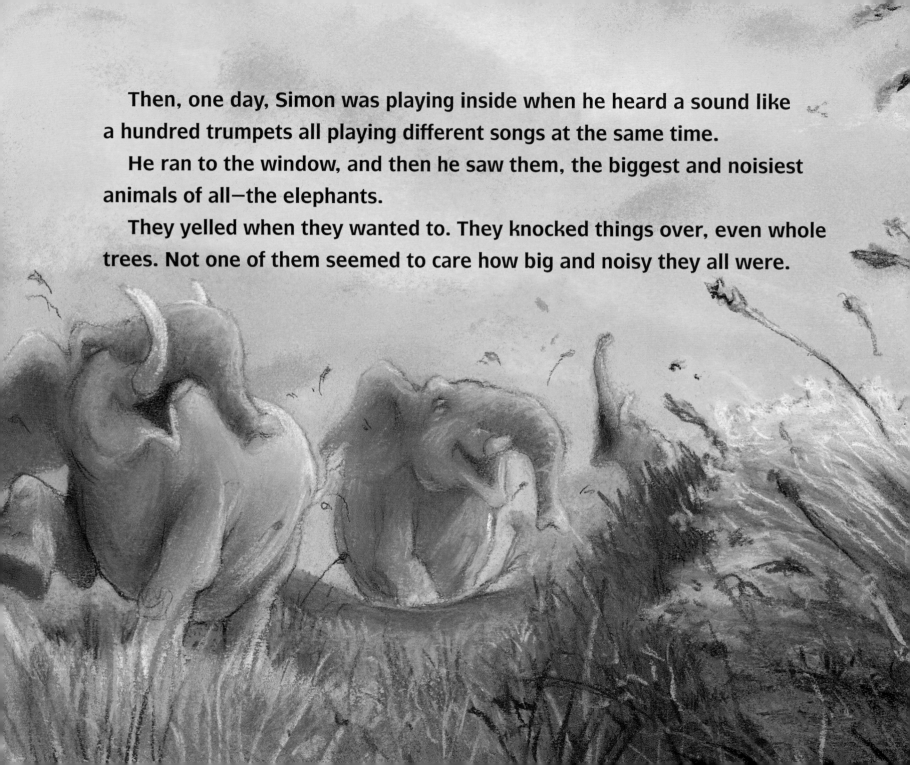

Then, one day, Simon was playing inside when he heard a sound like a hundred trumpets all playing different songs at the same time.

He ran to the window, and then he saw them, the biggest and noisiest animals of all—the elephants.

They yelled when they wanted to. They knocked things over, even whole trees. Not one of them seemed to care how big and noisy they all were.

That evening, Simon was as big and noisy as he'd ever been. He scared away the vervet monkeys.

He chased the guinea fowl.

He even knocked down a tree.
It felt great to be an elephant.

Late that night, something woke Simon up. He lay in bed, listening to the usual nighttime sounds. Then he heard something that sounded like people talking very, very quietly.

When Simon looked outside, he saw elephants. A whole herd of elephants, and they weren't making any noise.

The only sound was the whisper of the tall grass brushing against the elephants' sides as they moved slowly past.

Simon almost yelled for Mom and Dad and Annie to come see. But he didn't. He stayed where he was until the last elephant was out of sight, and all he could hear were crickets singing and an owl hooting.

After that, Simon couldn't stop thinking about the elephants. About how big and noisy they were sometimes, and how quiet they could be when they wanted to.

Simon thought about the elephants while his parents took pictures of gazelles, lions, and crocodiles. He thought about them when he was playing with Annie. He even thought about them on the plane ride home.

When the summer was over and school started, Simon found that he was still big and noisy . . . sometimes.

He was big and noisy when he was at a ball game or playing with his friends.

And sometimes Simon was still big and noisy when he didn't want to be. That was okay, too. Simon was sure that even elephants couldn't help being big and noisy . . . sometimes.

But most of the time, just as Simon was about to be big and noisy, he'd remember the nighttime elephants. He'd pretend he was walking across the dark savanna, and the only sound was the grass whispering against his smooth gray sides.

And then Simon knew
that he could choose when
to be big and noisy Simon,
and when to be just Simon.
Simon's mom and dad said
he was growing up.

But Simon knew he was
just being an elephant.